Mum,
I want to PEE.

Sharon Milling

Children's Fiction

First Printed in United Kingdom 2018
Published by Conscious Dreams Publishing
www.consciousdreamspublishing.com

Illustrated by Jason Lee
www.jasonmation.co.uk

Edited by Rhoda Moliffe

ISBN: 978-1-912551-14-9

DEDICATION

The book is dedicated to my beautiful, crazy daughter **Jasmine-Mae Milling.**

To my intelligent, beautiful son **TJ Bell**, stay as sweet as you are.

Jasmine woke up very excited this morning. She was going to the park with her mum.

She got herself ready, put on her shoes and danced around while she waited. Mum asked, "Have you been to the toilet before we go?" "Yes Mum," replied Jasmine. She was too excited about going to the park to even think about going to the toilet. So off they went to the park.

As they reached the park, Jasmine jumped up and down as there was so much to do there. There was a stage for all the shows, a big massive bouncy castle, people painting faces, a fun fair, a circus and even a farm with lots of animals. Jasmine was so happy that she wanted to see everything!

All of a sudden, Jasmine stopped and tugged at her mum. "Mum, I want to Pee!" Jasmine's mum looked at her and Jasmine shouted, "I WANT TO PEE!" Mum asked, "Did you not go before we left home?" "No," Jasmine replied, looking down at her feet. Her mum grabbed her by the hand and they walked so fast that Jasmine felt like she was flying.

They weaved in and out of all the busy people and exciting activities going on and walked all around the park looking for a toilet. They passed the circus and a clown was standing there ushering children in. Suddenly, he held Jasmine's hand to help her in. He tugged, she tugged, he tugged and she tugged again. Jasmine cried out, "I WANT TO PEE!" So he let her go.

At that instant, they saw the farm with a lady helping on the donkey rides. Jasmine's mum said, "We need to find a toilet and fast!" The lady said, "Jump right on and you will be there in a flash." Jasmine climbed onto the donkey and the lady led the way. The donkey was fast as it galloped through the park. "Toilets are this way," said the attendant.

The donkey ran straight through the face painter's tent. Everyone saw and ran in a panic. It was frantic in there. Everything was all over the floor. Jasmine turned and shouted, "SORRY!"

Then they reached the stage where children were dancing. The donkey ran to the front of the stage, took a bow then ran off the stage again. Jasmine gasped and shouted, "Not now donkey. I WANT TO PEE!" All the children watching started to laugh at the sight of the donkey.

The donkey jumped off the stage and onto the trampoline with a BOUNCE which lifted them both straight into the air. Jasmine screamed, "I WANT TO PEEEEEEEE!" They were so high they could see all of the park.

In a flash, they landed gently outside of the toilets and Jasmine ran inside. After she had finished, Jasmine's mum held her hand and said, "Next time, please go and pee before we leave the house." Jasmine replied, "Yes mum. That was fun. Can we do that again?!"

Lightning Source UK Ltd.
Milton Keynes UK
UKHW050717190819
348218UK00001B/1/P